TM

Note to parents, carers and teachers

Read it yourself is a series of modern stories, favourite characters and traditional tales written in a simple way for children who are learning to read. The books can be read independently or as part of a guided reading session.

Each book is carefully structured to include many high-frequency words vital for first reading. The sentences on each page are supported closely by pictures to help with understanding, and to offer lively details to talk about.

The books are graded into four levels that progressively introduce wider vocabulary and longer stories as a reader's ability and confidence grows.

Ideas for use

- Begin by looking through the book and talking about the pictures. Has your child heard this story before?

- Help your child with any words he does not know, either by helping him to sound them out or supplying them yourself.

- Developing readers can be concentrating so hard on the words that they sometimes don't fully grasp the meaning of what they're reading. Answering the puzzle questions on pages 30 and 31 will help with understanding.

For more information and advice on Read it yourself and book banding, visit **www.ladybird.com/readityourself**

Book Band 5

Level 1 is ideal for children who have received some initial reading instruction. Each story is told very simply, using a small number of frequently repeated words.

Special features:

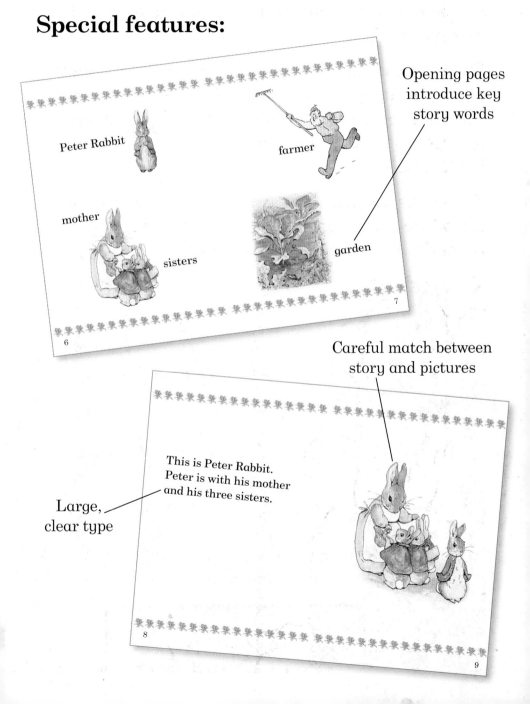

Opening pages introduce key story words

Peter Rabbit

farmer

mother

sisters

garden

Careful match between story and pictures

This is Peter Rabbit. Peter is with his mother and his three sisters.

Large, clear type

Educational Consultant: Geraldine Taylor
Book Banding Consultant: Kate Ruttle

A catalogue record for this book is available from the British Library

This edition © Frederick Warne & Co., 2013
New reproductions of Beatrix Potter's book illustrations
copyright © Frederick Warne & Co., 2002
Original text and illustrations copyright © Frederick Warne & Co., 1902
Frederick Warne & Co. is the owner of all rights, copyrights and trademarks
in the Beatrix Potter character names and illustrations.

Published by Ladybird Books Ltd
80 Strand, London, WC2R 0RL
A Penguin Company

004

ISBN: 978-0-72327-338-7

Printed in China

The Tale of
Peter Rabbit

based on the original tale
by Beatrix Potter

Peter Rabbit

mother

sisters

farmer

garden

This is Peter Rabbit.
Peter is with his mother
and his three sisters.

Peter Rabbit's mother said, "Don't go into the farmer's garden."

Peter's sisters went to get some berries for supper.

But bad little Peter Rabbit
wanted to get some
radishes. He went into
the farmer's garden.

Peter ate and ate.
He ate all the radishes
in the garden.
He ate so much that
his tummy hurt.

Oh no! The farmer saw
Peter Rabbit.

"Oh no!" said Peter Rabbit.
He ran away to hide.

The farmer ran after Peter.
But the farmer could not
catch him.

Peter Rabbit ran into
the shed to hide. But
then the farmer went
into the shed, too.

The farmer saw Peter!

Peter Rabbit ran out of the shed. Then the farmer ran out of the shed, too. But he could not catch Peter Rabbit.

Peter Rabbit ran out
of the garden.

Peter ran and ran.
He ran so much that
his tummy hurt.

Bad little Peter Rabbit
went home.

At home, Peter's mother
said, "Go to bed."
Peter Rabbit went to
bed with no supper.

And Peter Rabbit's three
sisters ate ALL the
berries for supper.

How much do you remember about The Tale of Peter Rabbit? Answer these questions and find out!

- How many sisters does Peter Rabbit have?

- What does Peter eat in the farmer's garden?

- Where does Peter go to hide from the farmer?

Look at the pictures from the story and say the order they should go in.

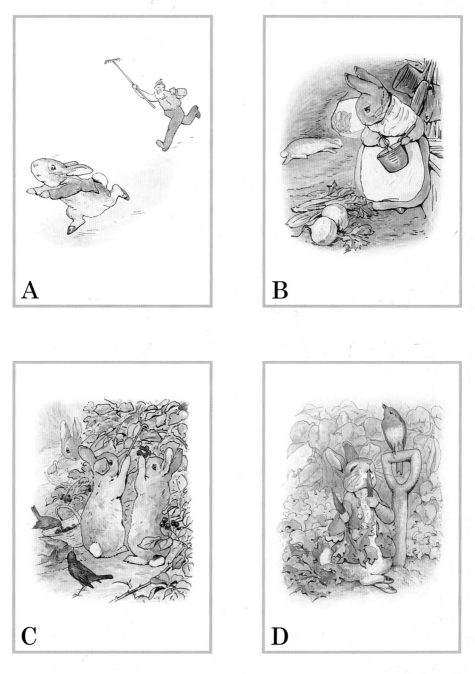

A

B

C

D

Read it yourself with Ladybird

Tick the books you've read!

Level 1
For children who are ready to take their first steps in reading.

Level 2
For beginner readers who can read short, simple sentences with help.

The Read it yourself with Ladybird app is now available for iPad, iPhone and iPod touch

App also available on Android devices